The Magic Black Belt

by Hanna Kim

illustrated by Emily Paik

STONE ARCH BOOKS
a capstone imprint

Published by Stone Arch Books, an imprint of Capstone
1710 Roe Crest Drive, North Mankato, Minnesota 56003
capstonepub.com

Text copyright © 2024 by Hanna Kim
Illustrations copyright © 2024 by Capstone

Library of Congress Cataloging-in-Publication Data is available
Names: Kim, Hanna (Children's author), author. ǀ Paik, Emily, illustrator.Title:
The magic black belt / by Hanna Kim ; illustrated by Emily Paik.Description:
North Mankato, Minnesota : Stone Arch Books, an imprint of Capstone, [2024]
ǀ Series: Ben Lee ǀ Audience: Ages 8-11. ǀ Audience: Grades 4-6.
Summary: Ben and his best friend are in tae kwon do camp, but Ben's lack of
confidence makes his awkward and embarrassed--until Mr. Wiz gives him a
magic black belt which seens to make him better, fast, but which may cost him
his friend.
Identifiers: LCCN 2023039081 (print) ǀ LCCN 2023039082 (ebook)
ISBN 9781669014416 (hardcover) ǀ ISBN 9781669017561 (paperback)
ISBN 9781669017486 (pdf) ǀ ISBN 9781669017493 (epub)
Subjects: LCSH: Tae kwon do--Juvenile fiction. ǀ Magic--Juvenile fiction. Self-
confidence--Juvenile fiction. ǀ Friendship--Juvenile fiction. ǀ CYAC: Tae kwon
do--Fiction. ǀ Magic--Fiction. ǀ Self-confidence--Fiction. Friendship--Fiction.
LCGFT: Novels
Classification: LCC PZ7.1.K57 Mac 2024 (print) ǀ LCC PZ7.1.K57 (ebook) DDC
813.6 [Fic]--dc23/eng/20230828
LC record available at https://lccn.loc.gov/2023039081
LC ebook record available at https://lccn.loc.gov/2023039082

Summary: Ben is nervous when his mom signs him up for tae kwon do.
Thankfully his best friend Emilio agrees to sign up too. But on their first day,
it becomes clear that Emilio is a natural. Ben, meanwhile, struggles to keep up.
He is frustrated and embarrassed—until he runs into Mr. Wiz, the custodian
from his school. Soon after, Ben finds a mysterious black belt in his bag.
Suddenly, his skills start to improve. Where did the belt come from? What's
behind the sudden improvement? And will the black belt help Ben come out
on top when he and Emilio face off? Or will it cost him his best friend?

Design Elements
Shutterstock: dawool

Designed by Jaime Willems

Printed in the United States   5815

TABLE OF CONTENTS

CHAPTER 1

TAE KWON DO SUMMER CAMP

"What even is tae kwon do?" I stared at the flyer Mom had pulled up on her laptop screen. There was a picture of a man in a white outfit with his legs kicked high in the air. The words *Tae kwon do Beginner's Summer Camp* stretched across the top of the screen.

"It's Korean martial arts," Mom replied. "You do kicks, punches, and all kinds of cool moves!"

Mom's eyes twinkled as if she expected me to jump up and down with excitement.

Instead, my stomach dropped. Kicks? Punches? I looked back at the picture on her screen. There was no way I would be able to do anything like that.

"Do I have to?" I asked.

"It will be fun," Mom said. "And it's only two weeks. It'll be good for you to try something active. And it'll help you build confidence!"

I sighed. Mom might be right, but I still couldn't help feeling nervous. This past winter, my dad's job had moved our family from California to a suburb in Michigan. The move meant a new house, a new school, and new friends.

I'd been nervous about being the new kid, but I'd survived my first semester at Andaleen Elementary. It had been a weirder start than I'd expected thanks to some mysterious lunch box magic.

After some of the other kids had teased
me on my first day, I'd made a wish to be
like everyone else. Suddenly everything
Korean had started disappearing—Mom's
cooking, my favorite TV show, gifts my
grandma had sent, and more.

Thankfully, I'd also made a new friend—
my neighbor and classmate Emilio. Turns
out, he'd had his own weird experience when
he was the new kid. He'd helped me stop
the magic from spiraling even further out
of control.

"Tae kwon do will be good for you, Ben,"
Mom said, bringing me back to the present.

Dad walked into the living room.
"My little Ben is learning tae kwon do?"
He pretended to wipe a tear from his eye.
"You know, I was actually pretty good at
tae kwon do when I was younger," he said
proudly.

Mom laughed. "Now you can barely touch your toes," she teased.

"Hey! I can touch my toes," Dad protested, crossing his arms. "Let me show you something very special." He walked over to the closet and took a box from the top shelf, then carried it over to me and took off the lid. "Ta-da!"

I leaned closer, and my eyes widened. The box was full of medals, trophies, and belts.

"Wow!" I said. "All of these are yours?"

I grabbed one of the trophies from the box. A figure at the top of the trophy was mid-kick. The words *First Place Advanced Tournament* were engraved on the base.

"Yep," Dad replied. "I told you I was pretty good." He stood up and did a few punches in the air. "Hana, dul, set, net!" he shouted, counting in Korean.

I had never seen my dad look so serious. He looked really cool doing the punches.

"Let me show you one of my most-prized possessions," Dad said. He reached into the box and pulled out a strip of plain black fabric.

I was confused. Out of all the trophies and medals, this was his most-prized possession?

"I know. It doesn't look like much, but trust me, it is." Dad rubbed his thumb gently across the fabric. "There are seven colored belts in tae kwon do. Each one represents a different rank. The first one is white. You get it when you start learning. You take a test to move on to a different belt. The next one is yellow, then orange, green, blue, brown, and finally black!"

I peered into the box to see the other belts. Together, they almost looked like a rainbow. Each belt had Dad's name, *Lee Tae Kyu*, embroidered on it in Korean.

"Okay, enough showing off," Mom said, nudging Dad. "What do you think, Ben? Do you want to give it a try?"

I looked at Dad's black belt again. Maybe I *could* give it a try.

"Can I ask Emilio if he wants to sign up too?" I asked. My friend would be coming over that afternoon to watch an episode of *Tobot V*, my favorite Korean show. "That's a great idea!" Mom agreed.

I smiled. With Emilio by my side, maybe I would feel a little more confident. Maybe tae kwon do wouldn't be so bad after all.

✦◆✦

"Hello, sam-chon," Emilio greeted Dad when he arrived that afternoon.

Dad waved before heading into the kitchen to help Mom make dinner. Emilio joined me on the couch. The *Tobot V* theme song was already playing on the TV.

A few seconds later, Mom came to the living room. "Good to see you, Emilio," she said. She set a tray full of orange slices and Korean shrimp crackers on the coffee table in front of us.

"Hi, e-mo," Emilio greeted her. He reached forward for a snack. "Ooh, shrimp crackers. My favorite! Thank you!"

I grabbed some crackers too. "Yeah. Thanks, Umma!"

"You're welcome, boys," Mom said with a smile before leaving the room.

Emilio and I watched TV for a few minutes. Onscreen, the main character, Pilsung, met with an alien robot. After, the commercials came on. I decided this was my chance.

"So . . . my mom wants me to do this two-week tae kwon do camp," I said. "It's Korean martial arts. I'm kind of worried about it. I've never done anything like that before." I hesitated. "Would you maybe want to do it with me?"

Please say yes. Please say yes, I repeated in my head.

Emilio grinned. "Definitely! I won't have soccer practice until later in the summer, so it'll be good training. I'll have to ask my mom, but I'm sure she'll say yes."

I let out a sigh of relief. Even though tae kwon do still sounded a little scary, it would be much better with my best friend there.

CHAPTER 2

FIRST-DAY NERVES

On Monday, Emilio walked over so we could go to our first day of tae kwon do together. I'd been so happy when he called and told me his mom had said yes. I still wasn't totally sure about the camp. But at least I knew I wouldn't be the only new student there.

"Tae kwon do is one of the best things I've learned," Dad told us on the car ride to the studio. "When you master all the skills, it starts to become a part of your natural routine."

Normally, Dad's bragging would make me laugh, but all I could focus on were the butterflies in my stomach. They seemed to grow as we got closer and closer to the studio.

"You okay, Ben?" Mom asked, looking at me in the rearview mirror. "You're awfully quiet."

"Just nervous," I said, fiddling with my fingers.

Mom reached back to squeeze my knee. "You won't know if you like it if you don't try."

I nodded. I knew she was right, but I couldn't help worrying about embarrassing myself.

"You and I are trying it for the first time *together*," Emilio added. "I'm sure it'll be fun!"

He put his fist out, and I bumped it with mine. Emilio had a way of easing my worries.

Soon we arrived at a small building with a sign that read *Kim's Dojang* over the door. Dojang, Dad had explained, was the Korean word for tae kwon do studio.

"All set, boys?" Dad asked.

I gulped. I didn't feel ready at all, but Emilio had opened the car door.

I guess I'm ready as I'll ever be, I thought. I grabbed my tae kwon do bag and climbed out of the car.

When we entered the studio, we heard loud shouts and stomping. "Hut! Hut! Ha!"

I held the strap of my bag tighter. It sounded a little scary.

"Now, boys," Dad said, interrupting my thoughts, "when you meet your instructor, bow low and call him Master Kim. It's a way to show respect, and that is an important part of tae kwon do."

Emilio and I nodded before walking down a long hallway. A tall older man, who I assumed was Master Kim, stood by a door at the end. He wore a white robe with a black belt tied around his waist. It looked different from any of the belts I'd seen in Dad's box. This one had five yellow lines and the word *sabumnim*—Korean for *master*—embroidered on it.

"See those yellow lines?" Dad whispered. "Each one represents a rank. There are five lines, so that means Master Kim is an oh-dan or fifth level. He's a tae kwon do master!"

Master Kim noticed us and waved. "Are you new students in our beginner session?" he asked. "We sure are!" Emilio shouted. "I'm Emilio!" I gave him a little nudge, and Emilio quickly bowed. "Master Kim," he added.

"Nice to meet you, Master Kim," I said, bowing too. "I'm Ben."

Our instructor chuckled. "Well, it looks like you both have the respect part down. Come on in! Let me give you your robes and belts."

Emilio and I turned to each other with wide eyes. We were getting our own belts!

We waved goodbye to Dad and followed Master Kim into the studio. A few kids, all dressed in robes and belts, waited inside. Master Kim went to his office and came out with two white robes. "Try these on and make sure they fit," he said.

Emilio and I kicked off our shoes and put them into the shoe rack in the corner of the room. Then, we slipped the robes over our clothes. They were perfect!

Master Kim pulled out two white belts. He wrapped one belt around my waist, crossing and looping it a few times until it became a super-strong knot.

"You will start with the white belt," he explained. "This means you are a beginner. By the end of the camp, you might even be able to earn a yellow belt."

"A yellow belt?" Emilio exclaimed. "I'm definitely going to get one of those!"

I remembered Dad's box of colorful
belts. Earning a yellow belt would be cool.
I hoped I'd be able to, but I didn't feel quite
as confident as Emilio.

Soon, we were ready to get started. Master
Kim stood at the front of the room.

Suddenly he put his arms next to him and
stood straight like a soldier.

"Cha-ryut!" he shouted.

We all stared at him, not sure what to do.

"Cha-ryut means *attention*," Master Kim explained. "Every time I say that word, you'll stand up straight and put your arms down as close as you can to your body. Let's try it!"

He showed us what it should look like. Everyone copied him.

"Great job," he said. "The cha-ryut position is a way to show respect. That's an important part of tae kwon do. In fact, it's part of the first tenet—courtesy. It's about being kind and respectful. There are five tenets in total. You'll learn about all of them in this camp."

Everyone nodded, and Master Kim smiled. "Good. You've already learned something. Now let me show you something more fun."

Master Kim put two fists up like a boxer. "Ha!" he shouted, punching the air.

Standing on one leg, he kicked straight with the other. He kicked a little higher, then higher still until his kicking leg formed one long line. To end, he ran from one side of the room to the other and did a flying kick.

Everyone gasped. Master Kim did the cha-ryut position and bowed. We all clapped.

"That was so cool!" Emilio exclaimed. "I can't wait to try it."

"Yeah," I replied. But secretly I was worried. How was I supposed to do any of that? I felt my hands getting sweaty.

"You'll actually be learning a few of these moves in this camp," Master Kim told us. "For today, we will start with a basic side kick. Kicks can be tricky. You need to make sure you have good balance and concentration." He kicked straight a few times. "See how straight I keep my leg?"

Everyone nodded. Master Kim's leg was as straight as a tree branch when he kicked.

"You also have to twist your body when you lift your leg." Master Kim demonstrated again. "Your arms should be bent near your chest with your fists closed. Now, why don't you all try? I'll come around to help."

I tried the kick Master Kim had demonstrated. It was hard to balance on one foot. When Master Kim got to me, I tried to extend my leg out as straight as I could.

"Not bad, Ben," he said. "But make sure to twist your body and raise your leg a little more."

I nodded quickly. I was glad when he moved on to the next student. I didn't want anyone to think I needed a lot of extra help. I was one of the only Korean students there. And my dad had a black belt. Tae kwon do should've come naturally to me.

"Ha!" I heard from behind me. I turned in time to see Emilio doing a perfect side kick.

"Wow, Emilio. Very good!" Master Kim exclaimed. He looked impressed. "Can you come to the front of the class to show everyone your kick?"

Emilio grinned from ear to ear as he walked to the front of the room. "Ha!" he shouted again. He kicked so hard I could hear the air *whoosh*.

Master Kim raised an eyebrow. "Are you sure you've never done tae kwon do before? You don't seem like a beginner."

Emilio shrugged. "I play a lot of soccer. I guess all the kicking practice helped."

I frowned. I should have thought about that. Emilio was obsessed with soccer. He was the center forward on his team. *It's one of the hardest positions to play*, he told me once.

Master Kim nodded. "Maybe you can help Ben with his kick," he suggested.

My face got hot, and I felt a pit in my stomach. Emilio was supposed to help me feel *better* about tae kwon do camp. He was a beginner too. But after seeing my friend's skills, I felt even worse.

✦✦✦

"That was so much fun! Wasn't it, Ben?" Emilio said on the car ride home.

"Uh-huh," I replied half-heartedly.

"What did you guys learn today?" Dad asked from the front seat.

"We learned how to do a kick today, and it was awesome!" Emilio replied.

He launched into a detailed explanation, chattering about how much he loved tae kwon do until we dropped him off. I wasn't surprised.

At home, Mom was already working on dinner. We were having jeyuk bokkeum—a spicy marinated pork dish. The smell filled the entire kitchen.

"Sounds like Emilio enjoyed today," Dad commented.

"What about you, Ben?" Mom asked as she worked on her spicy red pepper sauce. "How was your first class?"

I sighed. "I don't know. I don't think tae kwon do is for me."

Dad looked up from the fridge. "It's always hard when you try something new for the first time. How about we practice together after dinner?"

All I wanted to do was watch TV or read, but Dad looked so eager to help.

"Okay," I agreed.

After dinner, Dad got right to work. He held out a pillow. "Okay, aim for this."

I kicked weakly, wanting to get it over with.

"C'mon! Kick a little harder," Dad encouraged. "Put all your strength into it!"

I sighed. "Can we practice another time?"

Dad looked disappointed, but he put the pillow down. "Sure." He patted me on the shoulder. "But Ben? Keep your head up. Tae kwon do takes a lot of practice."

I nodded. Maybe Dad was right. Maybe today was just a bad first day. The next class would go better . . . right?

CHAPTER 3

KICK GONE WRONG

Master Kim stopped in front of me. "Ben, remember when I say *cha-ryut*, you have to put your arms at your sides."

I looked around at the other students. They were all in cha-ryut position. They were also staring at me.

My face burned with embarrassment. "Oh, yeah," I said. I quickly moved my arms to my sides.

It had been a few days since I'd started tae kwon do, and my skills had not improved. We had learned two new kicks. The first one was the roundhouse kick. It was tricky because we had to spin and kick at the same time. The second was the flying kick. It was even more difficult. We had to run, jump, *and* kick.

Most of the students, especially me, struggled with the two new kicks. Not Emilio, though. Master Kim called him up to the front of the class every day to demonstrate.

"You may relax," Master Kim said. Everyone relaxed their shoulders. "Today, I want to teach you about the fourth tenet of tae kwon do."

We had already learned about the second and third tenets. The second one was integrity—showing good character. The third was perseverance—not giving up when things get difficult.

"The fourth tenet is self-control," Master Kim continued. "This means you are keeping your emotions in check. It's about remaining calm and disciplined at all times. This will be especially useful today. You will be learning how to do a jab punch."

"I've never done punches before," Emilio whispered next to me.

Hope filled my chest. Emilio's soccer experience probably helped with his kicking skills, but neither of us had done any punches.

Maybe I'll be better at them than he is, I thought hopefully.

"Start by pushing your arm straight in front of you," Master Kim explained. "Make sure to look forward, not at your arm."

He showed us the punch a few more times. I was amazed at how strong and direct Master Kim's punches were.

"Now try it on your own," he said. "Make sure to put all your strength into it. I'll come around to check on everyone."

We began practicing. I recited the steps in my head as I did the movements. *Punch with*

*your arm straight. Look forward. Put all your
strength into it.*

When he got to me, Master Kim pulled
my arm forward a little more. "There you
go. Now you've got it," he said. He moved
on to Emilio next. "Excellent, Emilio!"

I frowned. Emilio was doing better than I
was—again! I tried a few more punches, but
what was the point? I would never be as good
as Emilio, not even at something I *should* be
good at.

I remembered what Master Kim said
about self-control. I had to try to not let my
frustrations get to me. But it wasn't easy when
my best friend was so much better.

"We will learn other types of punches in
the next class. For now, let's review our kicks,"
Master Kim said. "You'll each come to the
front of the room and do a side kick, aiming
for this target." He held up a small cushion.

I groaned inwardly. A kick in front
of the whole class? I was even worse at
those! Butterflies immediately filled my
stomach. I wanted to ask if I could go to
the bathroom, but it was too late. Master
Kim was already calling kids up to the front.

Emilio was first. He kicked right on the
target. It made a loud *smack*. Everyone
clapped.

"Very impressive, Emilio," Master Kim said.

The next student stepped forward, and I
tugged nervously on my belt. Each second that
went by made me even more nervous. Was it
too late to bolt out of the room?

Finally, it was my turn. "Ben, come on up,"
Master Kim said.

I slowly walked to the front of the room.
I could feel all eyes on me. I took a few deep
breaths.

Please let me do well, I thought.

31

"Ready?" Master Kim asked, holding out the target.

NO! I wanted to yell. But everyone else had already gone. *Just kick hard*, I told myself.

I got into ready position, then kicked as hard as I could. But I was so focused on kicking hard that I forgot to steady myself with my other leg. My standing foot wobbled underneath me, making me lose my balance and . . .

BAM! My entire body hit the mat on the floor.

Before I had time to understand what had happened, I heard snickers. I lay there, unable to move. I couldn't believe it. I had just fallen in front of the entire class—and now they were all laughing at me!

"Enough," Master Kim snapped, silencing the class. "This is new for everyone. That's why we practice."

But it was too late. I jumped up and ran out of the room. I sat on a bench in the hallway and angrily swiped away tears with the sleeve of my robe.

"I hate tae kwon do!" I spat.

"Ben?" a familiar voice said.

I looked up to see Mr. Wiz, my school's custodian, approaching. I sat up straight.

I'd had plenty of interactions with him at school, especially when all the weird stuff was happening with my lunch box. He always seemed to just . . . be around.

But I'd never seen Mr. Wiz outside of school—or out of his blue coveralls. Today he was wearing a white robe with a green belt tied around his waist. I caught a glimpse of the oval-shaped pendant he always seemed to have around his neck. It glowed bright yellow.

"Mr. Wiz?" I asked. "What are you doing here?"

"I've been taking adult classes here for the past few years," Mr. Wiz explained. He looked me up and down. "Looks like you're having a rough day."

I covered my face with my hands. "I just fell on my butt in front of the whole class. I'm so embarrassed. I'll never be good at tae kwon do."

Mr. Wiz sat next to me. "It's always hard when you learn something new," he said. Then he tapped a finger on his chin. "Have you learned about the five tenets of tae kwon do yet?"

"Yes, Master Kim taught us four of them so far," I replied.

"Good, good," Mr. Wiz said, stroking his beard. "I think the fifth one is the most important of all—indomitable spirit. This means that you have a strong mind and courage."

I nodded. I definitely had to work on some of those things.

Mr. Wiz put a hand on my shoulder. "The tenets take practice too, just like your tae kwon do skills," he continued. "You can't be good at everything from the start, but if

you have an indomitable spirit and keep trying, you will get better in time."

I sighed. It sounded a lot like what Dad had said. But I wanted to be good *now*.

"Well, I'd better get going," Mr. Wiz said, standing up. "But Ben?" He flashed me a toothy grin. "Maybe you'll learn this better if you learn it . . . differently."

Now I was really confused. "What do you mean?" I asked.

But Mr. Wiz didn't answer my question. He simply said, "I'll see you around," before turning and walking away.

CHAPTER 4

A SPECIAL BELT

"Are you okay?" Emilio asked me after class.

A couple kids leaving the studio smirked when they saw me. I felt my cheeks burn.

"I don't want to talk about it," I replied.

"Everyone is still getting used to the kicks," Emilio continued. "They come a little easier to me because of soccer. Maybe you just need some extra practice."

I knew Emilio was trying to comfort me, but it was making me feel even worse. Everything seemed so easy for him. "I said I don't want to talk about it," I snapped.

Emilio looked hurt, but this time he took the hint. He left me alone the whole car ride home.

As soon as Mom parked the car, I hopped out and ran up to my room. I threw my bag onto the floor and collapsed face-first onto my bed.

"Ugh," I groaned into my pillow. I couldn't stop replaying the fall in my head. The *BAM!* when I hit the mat. The concerned look on Master Kim's face. The laughter from the other kids.

Why can't I be like Emilio? I thought. *I'm the one who's Korean. Shouldn't I be a natural at Korean martial arts?*

Something sticking out of my bag caught my eye. I sat up and grabbed the bag, quickly unzipping it. There, tucked halfway in, was a black belt. But it wasn't like any black belt I'd seen before. This one had beautiful gold patterns embroidered into the fabric.

"Wow," I whispered. "Where did this come from?"

Maybe someone had accidentally dropped it in my bag? But everyone else in my class wore a white belt. I ran my fingers across the black fabric. I would give it to Master Kim tomorrow so that it could be returned to its owner. But for now . . .

It couldn't hurt to try it on, I thought.

I wrapped the belt around my waist and tried to tie it in a knot like Master Kim had shown me. Then I walked over to the mirror and stared at my reflection. I looked like a true tae kwon do master.

Maybe I'll try one kick, I thought.

I swung my leg out for a side kick. *Whoosh!* My leg snapped into position on its own.

"Whoa!" I gasped.

My form was perfect! The kick was so strong, it had even made a sound.

TOBOTV

I kicked again and again, and every time, it was perfect. The kicks were nothing like what I'd done in class earlier. I was perfectly balanced, and my leg was straight, just like Master Kim's had been. I was even able to quickly do a few in a row.

I stretched my arm out to do a cross punch. *Whoosh!* My arm shot away from my body.

"Hana, dul," I counted, doing two punches in a row. Each one felt strong and powerful. I couldn't believe I was the one punching.

"How . . ." I started.

I looked at my reflection in the mirror again. The only thing that was different was . . . the black belt. But the black belt couldn't possibly be the reason for my suddenly amazing skills. Could it?

I decided to test my theory. I took off the belt and tried a kick. My legs felt wobbly.

I quickly put the belt back on. When I kicked again, it was perfect.

I kept going, watching myself in the mirror. My punches and kicks looked as good as Emilio's—maybe even better. A smile spread across my face as I thought about showing off my new skills to everyone in class.

I had never believed in magic before I'd started at my new school. But after what had happened with my lunch box, I knew it was a real possibility. I didn't understand how I had gotten a magic black belt—or how it improved my tae kwon do skills—but it didn't matter. If this worked, I didn't care. I only cared that no one would laugh at me anymore.

"Ben, time for dinner!" Mom called from downstairs.

"One second!" I shouted back.

I glanced at my reflection once more before taking off the belt. I stuffed it under all the other junk in my bag. Then I went downstairs to the kitchen.

Mmm. The yummy smell of kalbi—Korean grilled ribs—filled the air.

"Do you want to try practicing some more tae kwon do with me after dinner?" Dad asked as we set the table.

Thirty minutes ago, I would have said no. But now things were different.

"Sure!" I agreed. "Maybe I'll even be better than you."

I crossed my arms and smiled, challenging Dad. With my new belt, anything was possible.

Dad chuckled. "You seem extra confident today," he said. "Just remember, I used to be a black belt."

He gave a kick to demonstrate, but his leg accidentally bumped against the table, knocking over the bowls and cups.

"Appa," I said with a face palm.

Mom groaned, rolling her eyes. "That's why you don't show off."

"Oops," Dad said with an embarrassed smile.

After dinner, I ran up to my room and put the black belt on under my shirt so Dad wouldn't notice. Then I met him in the living room to practice.

Dad held up a pillow again for me to kick.

"Okay, give me your best shot," he said.

I sucked in a breath. Would the belt work? I hoped so. I raised my leg and aimed.

"Whoa!" The impact of my kick sent Dad back a few steps. His eyes widened. "That was a strong kick, Ben!"

I put my hands on my hips like a superhero. The belt really was magic!

Dad ruffled my hair. "How did you improve so much?"

I hesitated. I knew the truth—it was the black belt. In a way, wearing it felt like cheating. But Dad seemed so proud. I didn't want to ruin the moment.

"I practiced extra hard," I lied.

"Well, it's paying off," Dad said.

He and I practiced a little longer. Every time I did a kick or punch, Dad looked surprised.

"I think that's enough for tonight," he finally said, putting the pillow down. He slumped onto the couch. "I need a break!"

I ran upstairs to my room and took off the black belt. Looking at it, I felt a little guilty. But wearing it was finally making me good at tae kwon do. That settled it.

"No more embarrassments," I said and tucked the belt into my bag.

CHAPTER 5

A LITTLE COMPETITION

The next day, I carefully tied the magic black belt under my tae kwon do uniform before I left the house. I didn't want anyone else to see it or ask about it. Emilio was already waiting outside. Together, we climbed into the back seat of Mom's car.

"Excited for camp today?" he asked as we drove.

"Definitely!" I exclaimed.

Emilio looked shocked.

Mom clearly was too. "Feeling better after your practice with Dad yesterday?" she asked, glancing back at me. "You seemed like a pro."

Next to me, Emilio turned and raised an eyebrow. I shrugged. I felt bad keeping something from my best friend. After what had happened with my lunch box when we first met, I knew he'd believe me. But I didn't want him to know I needed magic to be good at tae kwon do.

Mom dropped us off, and Emilio and I walked into the studio together. Luckily, none of the other students mentioned my fall from the day before.

Master Kim took his place at the front of the room and said, "Cha-ryut!" The whole class got into position.

"I have some big news today," Master Kim announced.

"At the end of camp, we will be hosting a beginners' demonstration. Everyone will participate to showcase what you've learned. There will also be a mock sparring match.

Today, I will be testing each of you on your skills. I will choose two students to participate in the match."

For a second, my stomach dropped. I didn't even want to imagine embarrassing myself again. But then I remembered my black belt. I balled my hands into fists. Things would be different today. I would make sure of it.

Master Kim had us line up. I stood behind Emilio. He practiced his punches while we waited. I played with the edge of my robe to ease my nerves.

Soon, it was Emilio's turn. He did a combination of jabs, uppercut punches, and cross punches. He also did some side kicks and roundhouse kicks. They were even quicker and stronger than before.

Master Kim gave an approving nod. "Great work, Emilio," he said. "Kicking comes so naturally to you."

Emilio beamed. "Thanks! I love the kicks," he said before sitting back down with the others.

I frowned. Did Emilio even realize he was showing off?

"Next!" Master Kim said.

I took a few deep breaths and moved to the front of the room. Everyone's eyes were on me.

Please work your magic, I silently begged the belt.

Closing my eyes, I let out a loud, "Hai-ya!" and raised my leg to kick in the air. *Whoosh!*

There was a moment of silence. My eyes were still tightly shut, expecting the worst. Then I heard cheering.

"Go, Ben!"

"Wow, that was amazing!"

"How did he do that?!"

I slowly opened my eyes. My leg was perfectly straight up in the air! My pose looked just like the one from the flyer Mom had shown me before camp started. Every kid in class—including Emilio—was clapping and cheering . . . for me!

Even Master Kim seemed impressed. "Wow, Ben! That was one of the best kicks I've ever seen," he exclaimed.

One of the best? A big smile spread across my face. I put my leg down and bowed a thank you to Master Kim.

"I have to say, Ben, I did not expect such a kick. You must've practiced very hard," Master Kim continued.

Again, I felt a twinge of guilt. I hadn't really been practicing much at all. "Why don't you show us some punches?" Master Kim suggested.

"Yes, Master Kim," I said. I got into the ready position and counted in Korean as I punched. "Hana, dul, set, net."

I did some jabs and even rotated my body to do a cross punch, one of the newer punches we had learned. My fists pushed out strong, even thrusts.

"Incredible," Master Kim said, his eyebrows raised with surprise.

I grinned and joined Emilio on the mat.

"That was awesome," he whispered. "I didn't expect you to do so well."

I immediately frowned. "What do you mean?"

"I just meant after yesterday," he said. "You got so good so fast."

My face got hot. "I practiced a lot," I lied, crossing my arms.

After everyone had been tested on their skills, Master Kim called for attention. "I am very impressed with all the hard work I've seen," he began. He looked at each of us thoughtfully. "Two students in particular have stood out and will participate in the sparring match. They are . . ."

I glanced at Emilio. I knew he would be chosen. He'd been the best since day one.
". . . Emilio and Ben! Congratulations!"

"Yes!" I cheered. This was the best day ever! I couldn't believe that only yesterday, I had been terrible at tae kwon do. Now I was one of the best students in class—all thanks to the magic black belt.

Emilio turned and high-fived me. "I'm so happy we both got chosen!" he said.

"Me too!" I said, forgetting Emilio's earlier surprise at my sudden improvement. This was what I'd imagined when I'd asked him to do tae kwon do with me—my best friend and I having fun together.

When class was over, Emilio and I hung out on the bench waiting to get picked up. As we sat there, Mr. Wiz came out of one of the other rooms. He wiped sweat off his forehead.

"Ben and Emilio!" he exclaimed. "How was tae kwon do camp today?"

"Great!" Emilio said. "Ben and I were chosen for the sparring match at the beginners' demonstration!"

Mr. Wiz looked at me and raised his eyebrows. "Oh, really? How exciting for you both."

"Sure is," I replied nervously. Yesterday, Mr. Wiz had seen me crying on the bench. I really hoped he wasn't suspicious.

"Well, congratulations to you both," said Mr. Wiz. He smiled at me. "And don't stop building your indomitable spirit, right, Ben?"

"Right," I replied. With a wave, Mr. Wiz walked toward the exit.

"What was that about?" Emilio asked.

I shrugged. "How would I know?"

"Hey, you should come over later tonight. We can practice together!" Emilio said.

My stomach twisted. I wanted to practice with Emilio, but what if he saw my magic black belt? "Um . . . that's okay. I think I might practice on my own," I mumbled.

Emilio's forehead crinkled with confusion. "Why? We could help each other," he said.

"I just don't want to," I said shortly.

Emilio looked hurt. I felt bad, but I couldn't risk having him find out about the belt. But my best friend wouldn't let it go.

"Are you okay?" he asked. "You're acting kind of weird. Is there something going on?"

Acting weird? I thought. *Why would Emilio say that? Does he suspect something?*

"There's nothing going on," I snapped. "You just want to practice together so you can prove that you're better than me."

Emilio's mouth dropped open, and he looked even more hurt. I crossed my arms and faced away from him. We didn't say a word to each other after that.

CHAPTER 6

A FRIENDSHIP DIVIDED

The car ride to our next class was silent. Emilio looked out his window. I played with the handle of my bag in an attempt to distract myself from the awkwardness.

Finally, Mom cleared her throat. "Excited for the demonstration?" she asked.

I'd filled her and Dad in on the event the night before. They'd been so proud when I told them, and they were excited to watch me spar with Emilio. With them watching, I had to make sure I won.

Neither Emilio nor I responded. Mom glanced at us in the rearview mirror, but she didn't say anything else.

Things didn't get much better between Emilio and I at the studio.

"Today we're going to practice the different moves we've learned so far in camp," Master Kim told us at the start of class. "Then we'll work them into a group sequence for our demonstration. That way your friends and family can see how much you've learned."

Master Kim walked us through all the different moves. The sequence would include a few side kicks, followed by a spinning roundhouse kick, and even a small flying kick. Then, we would move on to a mix of punches—a jab punch, an uppercut punch, and a cross punch. We would end with some ki-haps—shouts to show our energy and power.

"Okay, let's get into pairs and start practicing," Master Kim said.

Everyone started pairing up. Normally I would've practiced with Emilio, but things were awkward between us. Plus, I was wearing my magic belt under my uniform, and I didn't want Emilio to be suspicious.

Instead, I walked over to the corner of the room. I was going to practice hard and win the mock match. I began working on my jab punches on the wall mat.

"Good form, Ben," Master Kim said, complimenting me. "But don't you want to practice with Emilio? Maybe you can start preparing for the sparring competition."

I peeked at Emilio from the corner of my eye and saw him helping a few kids.

Hmph. He is such a show-off, I thought.

"I want to practice on my own today," I replied.

Master Kim raised an eyebrow but didn't say anything. He just nodded and walked over to another group of students.

I worked on my jab punches, then moved to the roundhouse kick. It was a tough skill. I had to move my hip sideways, kick out my leg, and then snap it back quickly. It would have been impossible without my magic black belt, but with it on, I did the kick easily.

After a few minutes, I decided to take a break.

"Can I get a drink of water?" I asked Master Kim.

"Of course," he replied. "There's a drinking fountain in the hallway."

I walked past Emilio. He was cheering on another student who was practicing a kick. I ignored him and kept walking.

In the hallway, I leaned over to get a drink from the fountain. The cool water felt so refreshing. Standing upright, I wiped the sweat off my forehead.

"Ben!" I heard a voice say from behind.

I turned and saw Mr. Wiz standing there wearing his tae kwon do robe.

"Hi, Mr. Wiz," I said.

He smiled at me. "Tae kwon do going a little better?" he asked.

"Yep," I said, smiling.

"Have you been practicing with Emilio?" he asked.

My smile immediately turned into a frown. "Not really," I replied.

"Hmm . . ." Mr. Wiz murmured, but luckily, he didn't ask more about it. "I've seen you a few times when I walked by your classroom. I'm amazed at how quickly you improved. It's almost like magic."

"Oh . . . yeah. I've, uh, been practicing really hard," I lied.

"I see," Mr. Wiz said. I caught sight of the pendant glowing under his shirt. "You know, I was thinking about our conversation from the other day. There's one tenet of tae kwon do that people often forget—integrity. If you're not honest, then you aren't able to show your true skills." He rubbed his beard thoughtfully.

Not honest? I thought. Was it possible that Mr. Wiz knew about the belt? I felt goosebumps form on my arms.

"W-what do you mean?" I stammered.

Mr. Wiz smiled. "Just reminding you of the tenets. Each one is there for a reason," he replied. "You should be heading back now. I'm sure Master Kim is wondering what's taking you so long."

That afternoon, Dad found me watching *Tobot V* alone on the couch. "Where's Emilio?" he asked, sitting down next to me.

"Not coming," I said. He'd made up some excuse about being tired. "What's going on with you and Emilio?" Dad asked.

"Nothing's going on," I mumbled.

"It doesn't seem like nothing. I heard you two didn't say a word to each other this morning," he said.

I shifted uncomfortably. "We sort of got into a fight," I said.

"A fight?" Dad said. "About what?"

I sighed. "About the sparring match."

Dad nodded like he understood. "Ah, good old competition, huh?" He stroked his chin thoughtfully. "Think about this, Ben. Are you having fun in tae kwon do right now?"

His question made me think. I was having fun. I liked being one of the best—maybe even *the* best—in my class. But I also missed my friend.

"I'm not sure," I finally replied.

"Don't you think you'd be having more fun if you and Emilio were talking to each other?" Dad asked. "You wanted him to do tae kwon do with you for a reason."

I sighed again. I knew Dad was right. Emilio and I were supposed to be doing tae kwon do *together*. But now that I had the black belt, did I have to choose between being the best or having a best friend?

CHAPTER 7

THE FINAL PRACTICE

The next week of camp was intense. Master Kim made sure we memorized every move.

"Practice makes perfect," he told us.

Unfortunately, things with Emilio were still icy. After my talk with Dad, I'd tried to find time to talk to my friend. But each time, I chickened out. I felt bad about what I'd said, but I didn't know how to make things right.

Finally, it was the last day of tae kwon do summer camp. The demonstration—and sparring match—were that weekend.

Emilio and I were practicing—separately— when Master Kim called us over.

"I noticed you two haven't practiced much together yet," he said. Emilio and I stared at the floor. "I think we should try sparring today. It will help you prepare."

I snuck a glance at Emilio. He looked uncomfortable with the idea. I was too. We hadn't talked since our fight. I also didn't know if I could beat Emilio, even with the magic black belt. He was a natural at tae kwon do. But Master Kim was right. We had to practice.

A few other students gathered to watch. Master Kim handed Emilio and me our body armor. It was only used for sparring, so I felt special putting it on. We donned helmets, chest guards, armguards, and leg guards.

Once we were suited up, Master Kim explained the rules. "In the actual demonstration, there will be a total of three rounds. Each round will last one minute," he said. "Your goal is to score as many points as possible in each round. You can earn points by landing a kick or punch to your opponent's armguard, leg guard, or chest guard. An attack to the head will lead to disqualification."

Emilio and I both nodded to show we understood.

"Today, we will do just one practice round. Anyone can start the first attack," Master Kim continued. "Since you two are beginners, you may only use jabs, cross punches, side kicks, and roundhouse kicks."

"Yes, Master Kim," I said.

Emilio and I bowed to our instructor, then to each other. We locked eyes for a second, but I quickly looked away.

"Cha-ryut!" Master Kim shouted, bringing us into the ready position. "Kyeong-rye!"

With that, the match was on. Emilio had a look of determination on his face as he slowly circled me. I hesitated, nervous about making the first move. Suddenly, Emilio charged toward me. *BAM!* He did a side kick and connected with my leg.

"One point for Emilio!" Master Kim said.

I tried to process what had just happened. *How did he do that so fast?*

"Good job, Emilio!" someone yelled.

My face turned hot. Even with my magic black belt, Emilio was beating me. But I wasn't going to lose so easily. I had a chance to prove myself, and I was going to take it.

"Yaaaah!" I shouted, running forward.

I spun my body for a roundhouse kick. *SLAM!* My foot hit Emilio's armguard.

Everyone gasped. Emilio stood frozen in shock. Then the kids started cheering.

"A point for Ben!" Master Kim announced. He walked over and put a hand on my shoulder. "Impressive roundhouse kick, Ben."

I felt like I was floating on air. Master Kim thought my kick was impressive! Even though I *had* done it with the help of my belt.

Emilio finally recovered. "That was awesome," he whispered. He gave me a thumbs-up. "Really."

"Thanks," I said proudly.

Master Kim calmed the class so Emilio and I could finish our match. I was able to get a few more points with some super-speedy punches and a few more high kicks. I also blocked and dodged Emilio's attacks with ease.

By the end of the match, I had scored ten points. Emilio had scored one.

"And the winner is . . . Ben!" Master Kim announced.

Everyone clapped. Several kids came up to congratulate me. Emilio came over too.

"You're really good at tae kwon do, Ben. A lot better than I am, that's for sure. You

were right. It was probably better that you practiced without me," he said sadly.

A pang of guilt filled me. I knew I wasn't *actually* better. It was the belt. I had been mean to my friend when he only wanted to practice together.

"Wait, Emilio—" I started to say. But Emilio was already walking away, his shoulders slumped in disappointment.

✦◆✦

"How was the last day of class?" Dad asked on the drive home. Emilio's parents had already picked him up. He'd said he wasn't feeling well.

"It was good," I said. "We did a practice match, and I won!"

"Wow!" Dad exclaimed. "Sounds like you're doing a lot better than I did when I first started tae kwon do."

"What do you mean?" I asked, confused. "Weren't you always good at tae kwon do?"

Dad laughed. "Not at all. I was the worst student in my class."

"No way," I said, shaking my head. The worst student? Dad had a black belt. I couldn't imagine him being the worst student.

"Yes way. I looked like a flopping fish!" he said. "It took me a long time to improve my tae kwon do skills. I had to retake the beginners' class three times."

My eyebrows shot up in surprise. *Dad* had retaken the class three times? I'd assumed he had been a natural at tae kwon do.

Maybe I should've tried practicing instead of using the magic black belt, I thought.

But then I shook my head. I couldn't think about that. I had a match to win.

CHAPTER 8

BELT DISASTER

The *Tobot V* theme song blasted from the TV. It was the day before the demonstration, and I knew that if anything was going to calm my nerves, it would be my favorite show.

Mom came into the room with a plate of sliced apples. "No Emilio?" she asked.

My stomach twisted. Mom had encouraged me to invite Emilio, but I still didn't have the courage to talk to him.

"No," I replied. "It's still kind of awkward between us."

Mom put the plate of apples on the coffee table and sat next to me. "Dad told me you two had a fight." She paused. "Do you know why I signed you up for tae kwon do?"

I thought back to when Mom had convinced me to go to camp. "So I could try something new?"

"Yes," she said. "But tae kwon do isn't just about learning punches and kicks. It's also about working on things like confidence, perseverance, and self-control. I know you want to do well, but don't let a little competition ruin a good friendship."

I bit and chewed on an apple slice. The *Tobot V* episode was playing in the background, but for once, I couldn't concentrate. Mom was right. I'd been so focused on being the best that I had hurt my best friend.

"I don't know what to say to make things right," I finally said.

"Maybe you can start by apologizing," Mom said.

I gulped. That was harder than it sounded. But I didn't want to lose Emilio as a friend. I would talk to him . . . after I won the mock sparring match.

✦◆✦

"Ben, hurry up!" Mom called up the stairs.

I quickly grabbed my things and shoved them into my tae kwon do bag, then looked around my room. *Do I have everything?*

"Ben, we have to go *now*!" Mom shouted.

I grabbed my bag and raced down the stairs. I couldn't be late for the demonstration.

"Got everything?" Dad asked.

"I think so," I said.

Mom, Dad, and I all piled into the car. Since they were also coming to the demonstration, Emilio's parents were driving him separately.

The demonstration was being held in a gymnasium close to the tae kwon do studio.

The whole thing felt very official. There were bleachers for family members and other visitors to sit and watch. I spotted Mr. Wiz sitting in the audience with some of the other adult tae kwon do students. He waved, and I waved back.

"We're going to find a spot," Mom said. "Good luck!" She kissed me on the forehead before leaving with Dad.

I searched the room for Emilio and spotted him in the corner, practicing with a few other kids. I put my bag away and moved to another mat to practice.

"Hai-ya!" I shouted, doing a side kick. I frowned. Something felt different. This kick didn't feel as strong as I remembered. I tried again. "Hai-ya!"

Something was definitely wrong. I patted my sides. Suddenly, I realized what was missing—my magic black belt! I'd been in such a rush to leave that I'd forgotten to put it on.

I hurried back to my tae kwon do bag and started searching frantically. *Where is it? Where is it?* I turned the bag upside down and shook everything out. The belt wasn't there.

"No, no, no," I said. My hands were shaking. I rummaged through all my things again. "It has to be here somewhere."

But no matter how many times I looked, the belt wasn't there. To add to my alarm, an announcement rang out from the speakers.

"Our demonstration will be starting soon!" a voice said. "Families, please take your seats. Students, please get into position for the group sequence."

Hot panic washed over my body. What was I going to do? I retraced my steps, hoping I'd just accidentally dropped the belt. I checked the main door, under the benches, outside of the gym. I looked everywhere, but the belt was nowhere to be seen.

I was about to go find Mom and Dad and ask them to check the car when the announcer's voice came over the loudspeaker. "Last call. Students, please get into position!"

I was out of time. I forced myself to take some deep breaths. Maybe I could just follow along with the other students for the group sequence. Maybe no one would notice if I made a small mistake.

As long as I find the belt before the sparring match with Emilio, I'll be okay, I told myself.

I joined my classmates at the front of the gym. My parents waved from the crowd. I tried to smile, but it felt like a lopsided grimace.

"Everyone ready?" Master Kim asked.

"Ready," the rest of the kids said.

We started with the three punches we'd learned: the jab, the uppercut, and the cross punch. I struggled a bit in the beginning, but luckily, I was able to follow along with the rest of the class. The audience clapped loudly when we were finished.

Then we moved onto a mix of side kicks and roundhouse kicks. The crowd oohed and aahed. I was surprised that I was able to do them all, even without my magic black belt.

I guess I picked up some skills during camp after all, I thought. When we finished, the audience clapped again. We all bowed. Master Kim smiled proudly as he faced us.

"Great job, everyone," he said. "Emilio and Ben, meet me up front for your sparring match. Everyone else can sit down."

Emilio and I exchanged a quick glance. Somehow, I'd managed to follow along with the routine. But during the sparring match, all eyes would be on Emilio and me. If I made a mistake, everyone would see.

I gulped. I didn't know how Emilio was feeling, but I was panicking. I tried to come up with an exit plan.

Can I sneak out and run away? No, everyone would notice. Could I fake being sick? I wondered. *No, Mom will see right through me.*

Before I could think of a better excuse, the announcer spoke again. "Our sparring match will start soon. Please remain in your seats."

Master Kim walked toward Emilio and me, gear in hand. "Let's get this match started," he said.

CHAPTER 9

THE FINAL MATCH

Emilio and I stood face-to-face. Sweat trickled down the back of my neck. Without my magic belt, I would lose right away. I was sure of it. What was I going to do? On top of that, I would embarrass myself. I could only imagine how disappointed Dad would be when he saw how terrible I was.

Master Kim handed us our body armor. "Make sure your punches and kicks are as straight as possible. Observe your opponent carefully. Stay alert the whole time," he said.

Emilio and I nodded and put on our gear, but I couldn't focus. The tension in the air was so thick. The only thing I could hear was my heavy breathing.

"I-I don't think I can do this," I blurted out.

Master Kim patted my back. "It's normal to feel nervous," he assured me. "Take some deep breaths and remember everything we've practiced."

I stared at the other kids. I looked up and saw my parents and Mr. Wiz in the crowd. Everyone was counting on me.

Master Kim stepped forward and faced the audience. "As promised, two of our best students, Emilio and Ben, will be taking part in a sparring match," he announced. "There will be a total of three rounds, each lasting for one minute. Emilio and Ben will compete with moves they've learned in class. Please give them a round of applause!"

The crowd cheered. Emilio and I bowed to Master Kim and then to each other.

"Cha-ryut! Gyeong-rye!" Master Kim shouted, signaling the start of the match.

I gulped. *Here goes nothing.*

Emilio and I got into the ready position. My friend's eyes darted back and forth. He seemed to be waiting for my attack. I wanted to start with a jab, but I didn't want to embarrass myself in front of everyone.

Emilio tightened his position and ran toward me. "Hai-ya!" Before I could dodge, Emilio hit me in the chest with a cross punch. "Oof!" I took a few steps back.

"Nice one, Emilio!" someone shouted.

We had just started, and Emilio had already scored a point! I had to do something before the round was over. I moved toward Emilio and raised my leg to kick, but he moved away quickly. My foot swished through the air and threw me off-balance. My standing foot slipped, and I teetered.

No, no, no. I tried to balance, but it was no use. I fell flat on my bottom.

The audience gasped. I heard a few kids chuckle.

I fought back tears. This was even worse than when I'd fallen in class. Now it wasn't just the other kids watching and laughing at me—it was *everyone*.

Emilio reached out a hand to help me. "Are you okay?" he asked.

My face burned with embarrassment. The last thing I wanted right now was Emilio's help. I ignored him and pushed myself up, refusing to make eye contact with anyone.

Master Kim blew his whistle. "The winner of the first round is Emilio! In thirty seconds, we will begin the second round," he said.

There was no way I could compete in the second round. The whole audience had seen me fall. I had to get out of there. Before anyone could stop me, I bolted for the door.

I kept going until I found a bench in an empty hallway. I sat down and covered my face with my hands. I couldn't believe I'd embarrassed myself again—in front of the entire audience!

The sound of footsteps startled me.

Great, I thought. *It's probably Mom or Dad.* I really didn't want to talk to anyone right now.

"Shouldn't you be inside getting ready for the next round?" a voice asked.

I looked up and saw Mr. Wiz. "There's no way I'm going back out there," I said. "Not after that."

Mr. Wiz sat down. "Every new skill takes practice. But you can never learn the new skill if you're too busy telling yourself you can't do it. Remember the indomitable spirit? You have to believe in yourself first."

Mr. Wiz had a point. I'd gone into tae kwon do already thinking I'd be bad at it.

"Why don't you try closing your eyes and taking a deep breath?" he suggested. I closed my eyes and tried to relax my body. I took a big, long breath. Suddenly, there was a flash of light.

"Huh? What was that?" I asked.

I opened my eyes and saw a tae kwon do studio. Only it wasn't my studio. The setup was similar, but everything looked unfamiliar. I spotted a calendar hanging on the wall. The date at the top read 1993.

1993? I stared in shock. *Where am I? What is happening?*

In front of me, kids practiced their kicks. A strict-looking man walked around the room, checking each student.

I looked around, trying to figure out what was going on. One minute I'd been sitting on a bench with Mr. Wiz and now I'd . . . traveled back in time? The strict-looking man walked closer to me. His eyes seemed to pass right over where I was sitting.

Can he see me? I wondered. *Am I invisible?*

The man paused in front of a boy who looked about my age. The boy was trying to do a kick, but he stuck out like a sore thumb compared to the other students. They were all doing their kicks easily.

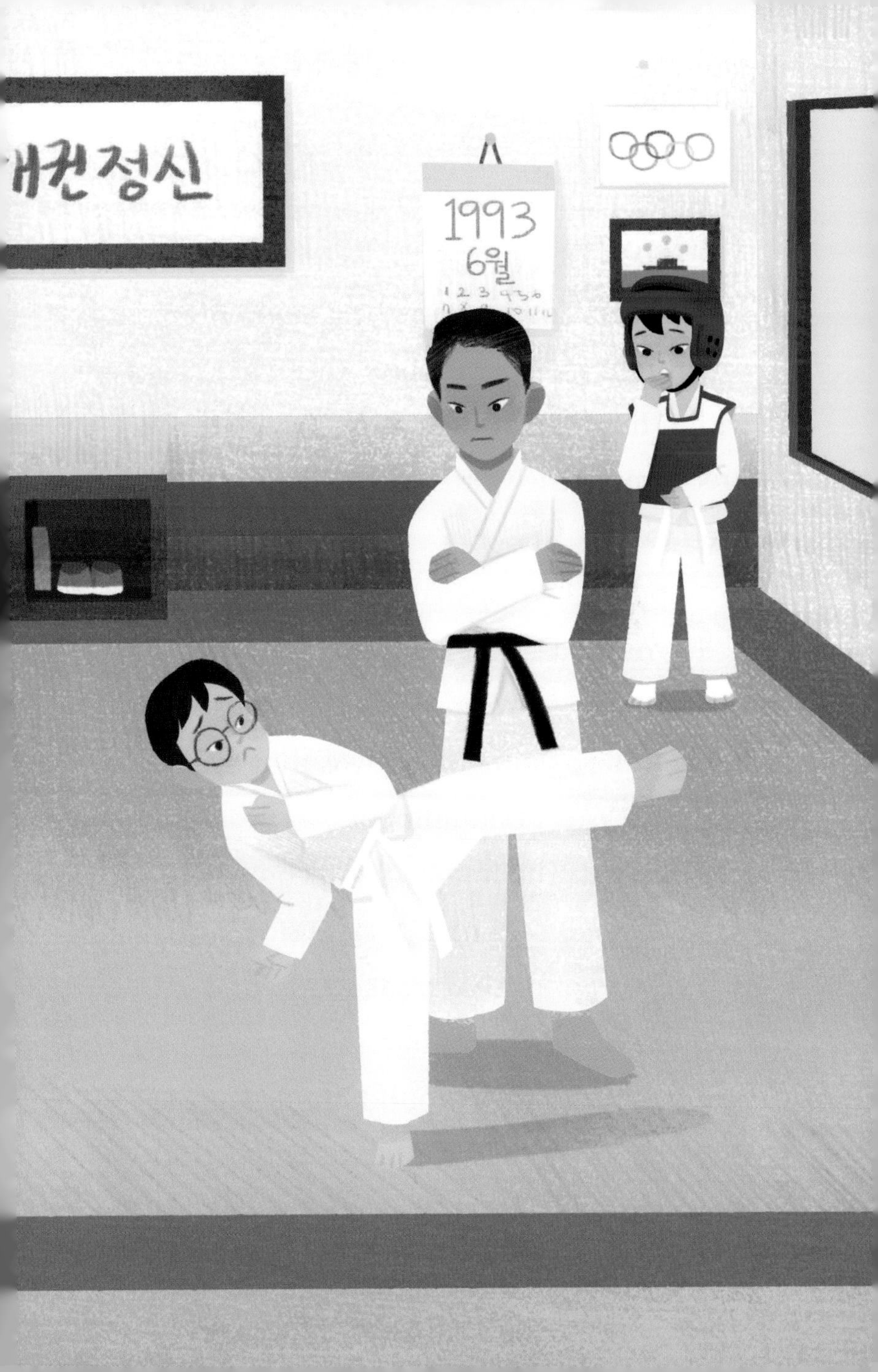
1993
6월

"Do it over and over until you do it right," the instructor said to him.

"Yes, Master Jung," the kid replied quietly.

I looked closely at the boy. Something about him looked familiar. Those kind eyes with a hint of mischief. Then I saw his belt. I recognized the words embroidered on it— Lee Tae Kyu.

"Appa?" I whispered.

It was Dad—as a kid! I stared at him, my mouth hanging open in shock. It was weird to see him so young. How was that even possible? Was I imagining it?

I blinked. The image didn't change. As I watched, Dad tried to do a side kick. But instead of raising his leg high and straight, he fell on his butt.

Some of the kids around him laughed. Dad's cheeks turned red, and I knew exactly how he felt.

"That's enough for today," Master Jung said sternly. "Pack up your things. Class is dismissed."

Everyone bowed to the instructor and started leaving the room. Dad, however, stayed. He walked over to a corner of the room and grabbed a mat.

What is he doing? I wondered. I wanted to walk closer and find out, but when I tried, I found I couldn't move.

To my surprise, Dad started practicing his kicks. They were as terrible as ever, but he kept trying again and again.

Finally, his instructor said, "That's enough. You can practice more tomorrow."

I watched as Dad tried one more kick. It was the best one he'd done so far. A big smile stretched across his face.

Suddenly, there was another flash of light.

"Ben? Can you hear me? Hello?"

I blinked, and things came into focus. I was back in the present, sitting on the bench with Mr. Wiz.

"What—" I looked around. "What happened? I saw my dad as a kid! I—"

Mr. Wiz didn't even flinch. "I don't know what you saw, but I see something different in you. Whatever it was, maybe it was supposed to help you gain the spirit to finish the match."

I tried to process everything I'd just seen. Dad practicing so hard to get his kick right. His determination. His refusal to give up. It had taken him a lot of practice to get to where he did. He definitely had an indomitable spirit. And now, I had a chance to show that I did too.

"You're right," I said, standing up. "I have a match to finish!"

CHAPTER 10

PLAYING FAIR AND SQUARE

Emilio was waiting for me outside the gym, his forehead creased with worry.

"Is everything okay?" he asked when I got close.

I nodded. "I'm okay now," I said, fiddling with the edge of my uniform. "Can I be honest about something?"

"Of course," he said.

"I know you're better at tae kwon do than I am," I blurted out.

Emilio looked shocked. "That's not true!

You were way better than me in our practice match," he said.

"It is true," I said. "I'll tell you everything later. But I knew you were better than me, and I was jealous. I'm Korean! I thought I was supposed to be better at tae kwon do than you are! I wanted to be better so bad, I let things get out of control. So, what I really want to say is . . ." I took a deep breath. "I'm sorry, Emilio."

My best friend was quiet for a second. "Is that why you didn't want to practice with me?"

"Kind of," I admitted. I knew Emilio would love to hear about the magic black belt—we'd both dealt with our fair share of magic this year. I would tell him all about it after the demonstration. "I shouldn't have blown you off like that. I really miss hanging out with you. Can we be friends again?"

Emilio's face lit up. "Friends! And I'm sorry if I was being a show-off. I can be kind of competitive when it comes to sports. I never meant to make you feel bad. I really missed hanging out with you too," he said. He held out a hand, and I shook it.

When Emilio and I entered the gym, I heard whispers everywhere. Everyone was probably wondering where we'd gone.

Master Kim hurried over to us. "Ben, are you okay? What happened?" he asked. He seemed a bit harried, like he'd been running around.

I felt bad. I'm sure our instructor had been worried.

"I'm okay. I needed a minute to think, but I'm ready," I said. Emilio and I smiled at each other.

Master Kim looked relieved. "Okay, good. Let's finish this match!"

Emilio and I took our places on the mat. I saw my parents giving me worried looks from the crowd and shot them a reassuring thumbs-up. I remembered the younger version of Dad, practicing until he finally improved his kick. I couldn't believe I'd been so worried about doing well when I'd only just started tae kwon do. I could only get better from here.

"Cha-ryut! Kyeong-rye!" Emilio and I snapped to attention and bowed. With that, the second match was underway.

I moved quickly this time, stretching my arm to do a cross punch toward Emilio's chest guard. I missed, but I recovered and got ready to attack again.

It's okay, I thought. *That wasn't a bad cross punch. I can try again.*

I circled around Emilio and went in for a quick jab this time. *BAM!* I hit his side.

Yes! I thought. *That's a point.* And I'd landed the jab even without my magic black belt!

There were only a few seconds left. I was doing a good job blocking and dodging Emilio's attacks, but he managed to land a roundhouse kick and earn another point.

I was impressed with how quick and powerful Emilio's kick was. He was definitely a strong opponent.

Emilio and I both tried to get another attack in, but the whistle ended the round. We had tied.

"Good job," I said, giving my friend a fist bump.

"You too," he said. "That jab was fast."

We rested for thirty seconds and then got ready for the final round. The crowd was fired up now. If I took this round, Emilio and I would be tied. If Emilio did, he would be the winner. I really wanted to win, but I knew I just had to try my best.

"Cha-ryut! Kyeong-rye!" Emilio and I started the third round.

We were both a bit tired, so our attacks were less aggressive. I missed a few punches, but I was also able to dodge a few.

Emilio managed to jab my armguard. I knew there were only a few seconds remaining. I glanced at Emilio. If I kicked perfectly straight up, I could probably land a side kick on his armguard.

I readied myself and then . . . *whoosh!* I heard a few gasps from the audience and looked up. My leg was perfectly straight in a side kick! But it had just missed Emilio's arm.

Fweeet! The whistle blew to end the match.

Emilio immediately gave me a hug. "That was a cool kick!" he exclaimed.

"I almost got you," I joked.

He laughed. "Almost."

Even though I hadn't won, I was proud of myself. I had competed without the magic black belt and still managed to score a point. And even though I'd missed, I'd done an awesome kick. Maybe being so worried had actually held me back from doing well.

"Gather around, everyone!" Master Kim called. All the students huddled together. "Excellent work, all of you. What a successful demonstration! I am proud of each of you for showing how much you've learned."

Our instructor put one hand on Emilio's shoulder and the other on mine. "And extra special congratulations to Emilio and Ben for being so brave and doing so well on their sparring match!"

"I'm glad I got to compete with you," I whispered to Emilio.

"Me too," he said.

Soon our parents made their way over to congratulate us too.

"Great job, boys," Dad said, giving us both fist bumps.

"I'm so proud of you!" Mom said, bringing us in for a big hug. "You both improved so much!"

"Can I sign up for more tae kwon do?"
I asked. "I need to practice if I want to be
as good as Appa."

"Of course," Mom said.

Dad beamed. "You're already better than
I was when I was your age."

I remembered Dad as a kid, struggling
with his kick.

"You might be right," I said with a laugh.

"Hey, don't get too confident," Dad joked.
"Go find your things, so we can head home."

I went to grab my tae kwon do bag, but
as I made my way back to my parents, I saw
Mr. Wiz. Something in his pocket caught my
eye—something black with gold embroidery
on it.

Is that . . .? I peered closer. It couldn't be my
belt, could it? How would Mr. Wiz have it?

Before I could approach Mr. Wiz, Master
Kim caught my attention. "We need to

celebrate," he announced. "Let's all go to Extra Scoops for ice cream!"

"Yes!" everyone shouted.

I turned back, but Mr. Wiz had disappeared. Shaking my head, I found Emilio, linked arms, and left to get some well-deserved ice cream.

GLOSSARY

aggressive (uh-GREH-siv)—strong and forceful

balance (BA-luhnts)—to keep steady and not fall over

concentration (kahn-suhn-TRAY-shuhn)—paying careful attention

grimace (GRIM-uhs)—a facial expression usually of disgust, disapproval, or pain

rank (RANGK)—an official position within a group

routine (roo-TEEN)—a part of a sports performance that is carefully worked out so it can be repeated often

rummage (RUHM-ij)—to actively search, especially by moving, turning, or looking through the contents of a place or container

showcase (SHOH-keys)—to exhibit especially in an attractive or favorable way

spar (SPAHR)—to practice fighting

tae kwon do (TAHY KWON DOH)—a form of Korean martial arts characterized by the extensive use of kicks

target (TAHR-git)—an object at which to aim or shoot

tension (TEN-shuhn)—a state of mental unrest that is often accompanied by physical signs of emotion

TALK ABOUT IT

1. Ben was hesitant to try tae kwon do at first. Have you ever tried a new activity? Talk about how you felt.

2. How do you think the black belt ended up in Ben's bag after class? Talk about your theories.

3. Ben and Emilio's friendship is put to the test during tae kwon do camp. Who do you think was right during their disagreement? How could they have handled things differently?

WRITE ABOUT IT

1. Ben was so embarrassed after falling that he almost gave up on tae kwon do. Write about a time something embarrassing happened to you. How did you handle the situation?

2. There are five tenets in tae kwon do: courtesy, integrity, perseverance, self-control, and indomitable spirit. Which do you think is the most important? Write a paragraph explaining your choice.

3. Imagine you could travel back in time and see a family member. Who would you want to meet? What would you ask them? Write a short story describing your experience.

MORE ABOUT TAE KWON DO

Tae kwon do is a form of Korean martial arts that has been around for thousands of years. It is different from other forms of martial arts, including karate, because tae kwon do uses more foot skills and kicks. The name comes from three Korean words. *Tae* means "to kick" or "to strike with the foot." *Kwon* means "fist" or "to strike with the hand." *Do* means discipline or art.

Tae kwon do officially became an Olympic sport in 2000. In a match, competitors score points by landing punches and kicks. All matches take place over three rounds lasting two minutes each.

Basic Tae Kwon Do Moves and Commands

- **bah ro**—back to ready position
- **cha-ryut**—attention; hands at side and feet close together, facing the instructor
- **cross punch**—a punch done while rotating the body
- **flying kick**—a kick that requires running, then kicking while jumping
- **go mahn**—stop
- **jab punch**—a quick, snappy punch

- **joon bee**—ready position
- **ki-hap**—yell
- **kyung nae**—bow; hands at side while bowing at a 90-degree angle
- **roundhouse kick**—a kick done while spinning
- on one foot
- **shee jak**—start/begin
- **shee uh**—at east/rest
- **side kick**—a basic kick straight to the side
- **uppercut punch**—an underhand punch with legs spread apart

Tae Kwon Do Belt Levels

Tae kwon do uses belt colors to show someone's level or rank. The word *geup* means degree. At the black belt level, the word *dan*—meaning phase—replaces gup/geup. World Taekwondo, the international federation governing the sport, has 11 ranks:

- 11th geup—white belt
- 10th geup—yellow belt
- 9th geup—orange belt
- 8th geup—green belt
- 7th geup—purple belt
- 6th geup—blue belt
- 5th geup—blue and black belt
- 4th geup—brown belt
- 3rd geup—brown and black belt
- 2nd geup—red belt
- 1st geup—red and black belt
- 1st dan—black belt

ABOUT THE AUTHOR

Hanna Kim is the author of the Ben Lee series. She is also a middle school English language arts teacher. She was inspired to write this story because of her dad, who learned tae kwon do when he was younger. In her free time, Hanna loves to draw, read, make fun crafts, and eat Korean snacks. She lives in Michigan with her husband and cat, Zoro.

Photo credit: Milan Puscas

ABOUT THE ILLUSTRATOR

Emily Paik is an illustrator who lives in South Korea with two dogs, Tofu and Doona. She loves to go on adventures with her dogs and gets inspired by the colors and shapes of nature. She hopes to create illustrations that will warm people's hearts and make them smile.

Photo credit: Emily Paik